DON'T ENTER THE HOUSE!

Veronika Martenova Charles
Illustrated by David Parkins

Tundra Books

Published in Canada by Tundra Books,
75 Sherbourne Street, Toronto, Ontario M5A 2P9

Published in the United States by Tundra Books of Northern New York,
P.O. Box 1030, Plattsburgh, New York 12901

Library of Congress Control Number: 2008900097

Library and Archives Canada Cataloguing in Publication

Charles, Veronika Martenova
Don't enter the house! / Veronika Martenova Charles ; illustrated by David Parkins.

(Easy-to-read spooky tales)
ISBN 978-0-88776-856-9

1. Horror tales, Canadian (English). 2. Children's stories, Canadian (English).
I. Parkins, David II. Title. III. Series: Charles, Veronika Martenova. Easy-to-read spooky tales.

PS8555.H42242D553 2008 jC813'.54 C2007-907593-2

We acknowledge the financial support of the Government of Canada through the Book Publishing Industry Development Program (BPIDP) and that of the Government of Ontario through the Ontario Media Development Corporation's Ontario Book Initiative. We further acknowledge the support of the Canada Council for the Arts and the Ontario Arts Council for our publishing program.

Printed and bound in Canada

1 2 3 4 5 6 13 12 11 10 09 08

CONTENTS

BIKE RIDE

PART 1

"Let's go for a bike ride,"

I said to Leon and Marcos.

We got on our bikes and

took the road around the lake.

We came to a big house

with a *For Sale* sign.

"That house has been empty

for a long time," said Marcos.

"Maybe it's haunted," I said.

A sign on the front porch read:

Private. Don't Enter the House!

We got off our bikes

and walked around the house.

"I wonder what it's like inside,"

said Leon.

"Look! There's a broken window.
Let's climb in," Leon suggested.
"I don't think we should," I said.
"But nobody lives here," said Leon.
"Maybe we'll find a treasure."
We climbed through the window.
Inside were a few broken chairs
and some rat traps.
We went upstairs.
"Look at this!" I said.
Someone had drawn on the wall.

"What do you think it is?" I asked.

"It looks like a cat," said Marcos.

"We better watch out for the giant rat!"

Leon whispered.

"Why?" asked Marcos.

"I'll tell you a story," said Leon.

THE BOY WHO DREW CATS

(Leon's Story)

Once there was a boy

who liked to draw cats.

He was curious and clever,

so his father asked their priest

if the boy could become

his student.

The old man agreed and invited

the boy to live at the temple.

But the boy didn't study.

Instead, he drew pictures of cats

inside his books and on the walls.

The priest was not pleased.

"I cannot keep you as a student.

You must pack your things and go.

But take my advice:

Avoid the large places at night.

Keep to the small."

The boy was too upset to ask

what the old man meant.

The next morning,

the boy left the temple.

He was afraid to tell his father

that he had failed,

so he started walking

to the next village.

On the way, he came to a large house.

On the gate was a sign:

Don't Enter the House!

The boy was tired, so he knocked.

When nobody answered,

he pushed the gate and it opened.

Inside, the walls were white.

The boy could not resist.

He drew cats everywhere.

Big cats, small cats,

cats jumping, cats sleeping.

Hundreds of cats were now

all over the walls.

Outside, it was growing dark.

The boy decided to spend

the night in the house.

Suddenly, he remembered

what the old priest had told him:

Avoid the large places at night.

Keep to the small.

He still didn't know what it meant,

but he searched for a place to hide.

The boy found a small cupboard

and squeezed himself inside.

In the middle of the night
he was awakened by sounds.
Something was inside the house,
gliding across the floor.
It was sniffing and scratching
at the cupboard door,
trying to pull it open.
The whole house filled
with screams and howls.
It sounded like a battle.
Suddenly, the noise stopped!

The boy waited until daylight

shone through a crack.

Then he crawled out of the cupboard.

The floor was covered

with mud and fur.

A giant rat, as big as an elephant,

lay there – dead!

What happened?

Who was fighting in the night?

The boy looked at the walls.

The cats were all in different places.

They were much bigger than before.

Now the boy knew

why there was the sign,

Don't Enter the House!

and why the priest had told him,

Avoid the large places at night.

Keep to the small.

That day, the boy returned home.

In time he became a famous artist.

"I don't think the drawing

on this wall *is* a cat," said Marcos.

"Well, if it is, maybe this house

is haunted too," I said.

"That's why nobody has bought it."

I looked out the window.

There were waves on the lake.

They made me think of something

I had heard.

"Can I tell you another

haunted house story?" I asked.

"Sure," Leon and Marcos replied.

THE HAUNTED BEACH HOUSE

(My Story)

Sara, Lyn, and Kate were classmates.

Lyn and Kate lived in town,

while Sara lived in a beach house

with her father.

One day, Sara didn't come to school.

She was gone for a whole week.

"Where is Sara?"

Lyn asked the teacher.

"She went on a fishing trip

with her dad," the teacher replied.

Lyn whispered to Kate,

“That’s strange, because I saw Sara

on the way to school.

I called to her, but she ignored me.

Maybe we should visit her

and find out what’s going on.”

After school the two friends
walked to Sara's beach house.
A sign was taped on the door.
It said: *Don't Enter the House!*
"Some welcome," said Kate.
"I guess we should go home."

"No!" said Lyn.

"We're here, and I want to see her."

Lyn knocked on the door.

There was no response.

"I don't think Sara is home,"

said Kate. "Let's look

through the window."

The girls peeked in,

but they didn't see anyone.

There was another door inside.

A light shone under it.

Suddenly, the door swung open.

There was Sara,

standing with her eyes closed.

She slowly crossed the room

and unlocked the front door.

Lyn and Kate entered,

but Sara had vanished.

"What is Sara doing?" asked Lyn.

"Why is she hiding on us?"

"Maybe we should leave," said Kate.

Lyn called, "Sara! Come out!

We want to say hello!"

The room filled with the smell of the ocean, and water began to seep under the front door. The girls stepped back.

SWOOSH!

A huge wave burst through the door and left the girls soaking wet.

A voice came from the other room.

“I knew you would come.

I will take you for a swim!”

The girls screamed and ran outside.

They kept running until

they reached the town.

When they got home,

their parents told them

that Sara and her father

never returned from their trip.

Only their boat was found . . . empty.

"That's sad," said Leon.

"I guess Sara became a ghost.
Is that story true?" he asked.

"There are no ghosts," I said.
"They're just make-believe."

"I also know a story about
a scary house and a father
who's a fisherman," said Marcos.

"Tell us!" Leon said.
"Then we'll go biking again."

THE MOUNTAIN WITCH

(Marcos' Story)

There once was a boy called Kaito.

His father was a fisherman.

When the father could no longer

sell fish in their village, Kaito said,

"I'll take the fish to the village

market beyond the mountains.

I'll go tonight when it's cool,

and I'll be there early.

That way I'll get the best price."

"Be careful!" said his father.

"People say that a witch lives

in a house in the mountains.

If you see it, *don't enter the house!*"

That evening,

Kaito took a barrel of fish

and set off for the mountains.

The way was steep.

Kaito climbed higher and higher

up the moonlit path.

Suddenly, the boy heard footsteps.

He looked back and saw a woman.

She had a horrible face.

Kaito shivered.

This must be the mountain witch,

he thought.

He walked faster,

but the woman followed him.

He ran, but she ran too.

Then the witch called out,

"Give me your fish. I'm hungry!"

"I can't," Kaito answered.

"I'm taking the fish to market!"

"THEN I'LL EAT YOU FIRST,"

the witch screamed,

"AND JUST TAKE THE FISH!"

Her mouth was full

of huge, sharp teeth.

Kaito dropped the barrel and fled into the woods. *If only I could find a safe place to spend the night*, he thought.

Among the trees he saw a light.

It was coming from a small house.

Good, this must be the home

of a woodcutter, he thought.

Kaito knocked on the door.

"Is anybody home?"

There was no answer.

Kaito opened the door.

“Is anybody here?” he called.

Nobody came to welcome him,

but Kaito was too tired to care.

He entered, climbed upstairs,

and fell asleep.

Some time later,

a voice downstairs woke him.

The woodcutter must be home,

Kaito thought, and started

down the stairs to meet him.

But halfway down, he realized

the voice was the old woman's.

"What a lovely dinner I had.

A whole barrel of fish!" she sang.

Oh, no! Kaito thought.

This is NOT a woodcutter's house.

IT BELONGS TO THE

MOUNTAIN WITCH!

BIKE RIDE
PART 2

"Sh!" said Leon.

The door downstairs squealed

and someone entered the house.

Maybe it's the witch, I thought.

"What do we do now?" asked Leon.

"We're trapped!"

"Let's hide," I said.

There was an old cupboard.

We opened it and squeezed inside.

It smelled of dust and rotten wood.

We could hear a woman's voice.

She was mumbling something.

Next, we heard footsteps.

They were getting nearer.

They entered the room.

Something ran across the floor.

It sniffed and clawed at our door.

Marcos grabbed my arm.

"It must be THE GIANT RAT!!"

I held my breath.

Dust tickled in my nose –

"ATCHOOO!!!"

"What was THAT?"

the woman's voice said.

Suddenly, the cupboard door

flew open.

The light hit our eyes.

"AHHH!" someone screamed.

"AHHH!" screamed Leon and Marcos.

A woman and a dog stared at us.

"What are you doing here?"

shouted the woman.

"Didn't you read the sign?

This is private property,

not a playground.

I don't want to find you

here again, understand?"

"Yes!" we said,

and scrambled outside.

"I knew we shouldn't

have gone in that house,"

I told Leon and Marcos.

"That lady was not very nice,"

said Marcos.

"Maybe she *is* a witch,"

said Leon.

We quickly got on our bikes

and rode home.

AFTERWORD

What do you think happened to Kaito in *The Mountain Witch*? Do you think the old woman caught him? Can you think of how he might have escaped?

WHERE THE STORIES COME FROM

Worldwide, there are folktales

in which people are warned

not to enter a certain house.

They enter the house anyway,

because they don't listen,

are curious, or simply forget.

The Boy Who Drew Cats and

The Mountain Witch are based on

folktales from Japan.

The Haunted Beach House

comes from California, U.S.A.